JAKE MADDOX
GRAPHIC NOVEL

D0516745

HOME ICE
RIVALS

STONE ARCH BOOKS
a capstone imprint

JAKE MADDOX
GRAPHIC NOVELS

Published by Stone Arch Books,
an imprint of Capstone.
1710 Roe Crest Drive
North Mankato, Minnesota 56003
www.capstonepub.com

Copyright © 2021 by Capstone. All rights reserved.
No part of this publication may be reproduced in
whole or in part, or stored in a retrieval system, or
transmitted in any form or by any means, electronic,
mechanical, photocopying, recording, or otherwise,
without written permission of the publisher.

Library of Congress Cataloging-in-Publication Data
is available on the Library of Congress website.

ISBN: 978-1-4965-9710-6 (library binding)
ISBN: 978-1-4965-9921-6 (paperback)
ISBN: 978-1-4965-9756-4 (ebook PDF)

Summary: Benny Krueger loves playing hockey with
his friends on the lake by his home. So when his
parents announce that they have to move, it breaks
his heart. Even worse, Benny's older sister loves to
embarrass him at the rink. When he learns about a
pond hockey tournament being held near his house,
he rallies his friends to take on his sister's team.
Will Benny finally defeat his sister and gain some
confidence in his own skills on the ice?

Editor: Aaron Sautter
Designer: Cynthia Della-Rovere
Production Specialist: Tori Abraham

Printed in the United States of America.
PA117

HOME ICE RIVALS

Text by Brandon Terrell

Art by Roberta Papalia

Lettering by Jaymes Reed

Cover Art by Berenice Muñiz

HOME ICE
RIVALS

BENNY KRUEGER

RAINA KRUEGER

BENNY'S PARENTS

TAM RODRIGUEZ

THE TEAM

Summer here at my house is one long vacation.

What a perfect day.

Mffph. To-mffph-tally.

I love those long summer days. But as much as I love swimming and goofing around with my friends . . .

. . . a Minnesota winter on the lake is even better.

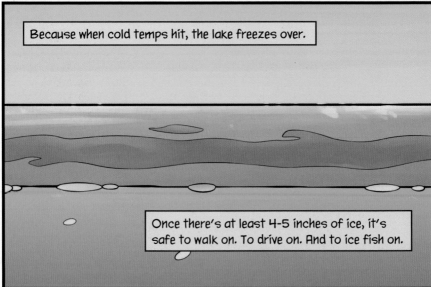

Because when cold temps hit, the lake freezes over.

Once there's at least 4-5 inches of ice, it's safe to walk on. To drive on. And to ice fish on.

More than that, though, it's safe for . . .

. . . playing pond hockey!

Nothing's better than playing on the ice with my friends.

Every day we're skating across the makeshift rink outside my house.

And the brilliant Benny Krueger brings the puck across the blue line!

Nothing stands in his way.

Except his best friend and defensive wizard Tam!

THUMP!

Ugh. My older sister, Raina, has spent her whole life bragging about being better at stuff than me.

See, Benny's good and all. But I'm in a league all my own.

She doesn't realize she's doing it, either.

SWAT!

Nice try, squirt.

She just says things without thinking about my feelings.

Look, I got a B+ in advanced algebra!

Oh. I remember that class. I got an A.

Plus, she loves to remind me that she's older and bigger than me.

One day you'll be able to reach the top shelf, little bro.

See what I mean? Raina's a great player. But she can be a bit much.

And of course, I never just let it go. I stew. Sulk. Grumble.

Benny! Raina! Dinner!

That evening I'm still stewing about her showing me up on the ice.

That is, until I see . . .

Oh no . . .

It's Mom's special creation—Bad News Meatloaf.

She only makes it when she and Dad have special news. But it's usually news that upsets my sister and me.

The delicious meatloaf is meant to distract us.

Of course, I'm the only one who's caught on to Mom's trick. Raina's clueless.

Out of the way, squirt.

Oooh. Meatloaf. Yum.

THUMP!

A new house? That's . . .

That's awesome!

Do you think we could move to the Edgewater district?

They have the best hockey team. I could try out, make the team, and—

Whoa there, Raina. We're just starting the process.

But we love your enthusiasm, dear.

Benny? You're so quiet. How do you feel about this?

I mean . . . a baby. That's um, great. But moving?

We can't move.

The fog was clearing in my head, and it was all coming into focus.

I already feel left out and forgotten when Raina is around. But now, with the baby too?

My parents will never pay attention to me.

I love this house. I love the lake. And I don't wanna lose it!

Benny? Honey, please stop. Let's talk about it.

No! Everyone just leave me alone!

I don't want to talk to anyone. I especially don't want to deal with the fallout from the Bad News Meatloaf.

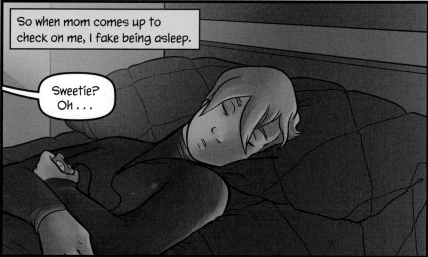

So when mom comes up to check on me, I fake being asleep.

Sweetie?
Oh . . .

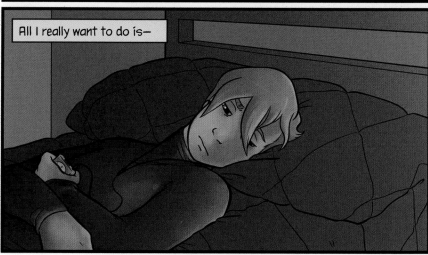

All I really want to do is—

29

That's parents for you. It's what they do.

Well, this conversation, and this movie, are bringing me down.

Let's go do something fun.

CLICK!

I have an idea.

Because when I'm with my friends—

Benny! I'm open!

—I don't have to stand out like my sister.

Instead, I'm part of a team.

SWISH!

And I can take my mind off all of the stuff going on at home. Raina. The baby. The house.

THWACK!

None of that matters when I'm on the ice.

FSH!

Nice shot, Cora.

Thanks, dude.

It was a beautiful evening. We could have played all night.

But eventually, Ryan's stomach had other ideas . . .

A pond hockey tournament—on Prairie Lake!

Raina had mentioned it last week. She and her friends were signing up for the junior division.

If we could just beat her team . . .

COMMUNITY EVENTS

DOG ADOPT

1ST ANNUAL PRAIRIE LAKE POND HOCKEY TOURNAMENT!

VERY IMPOR

SIGN UP NOW!

That'll be $12.57.

This is it, guys! We should totally sign up for this!

COMMUNITY EVENTS

DOG ADOPT

1ST ANNUAL PRAIRIE LAKE POND HOCKEY TOURNAMENT!

VERY IMPOR

GN UP NOW!

Cool.

I'm down with it.

I can't explain to my friends why I'm so excited. Can't tell them how much I want to beat my sister and prove to my parents that I'm just as good as she is.

RIIIPP!

1ST ANNUAL PR LAKE POND H TOURNAMEN

All right. The form's filled out and turned in. We're officially in the tournament. Now who's ready to practice?

The tournament is a month away, so we practice every chance we get, no matter what the weather hands us.

CRACK!

We practice in the freezing cold.

We practice in snowstorms.

After all, that's what makes pond hockey so cool.

Because we play outside, we have to be prepared for any type of weather.

WHOOSH!

And we're gonna do everything we can to win that tournament and take my sister's team down.

While they're downstairs being all happy and stuff, I'm upstairs scouting bedrooms.

Ha. We knew you'd find that info exciting. Now where's your brother?

I'm right here.

If we're going to buy this house, I call dibs on the bedroom at the end of the hall.

No, I don't agree. But they aren't going to take my side. They always take her side.

So it isn't worth arguing.

Whatever. Then I'll take the one with the two big windows.

Ooh . . . we'll see, sweetie. That room is the closest to ours.

Your father and I thought it would be the best room for the nursery.

. . . sigh . . .

Sure, fine. I'll be in the car.

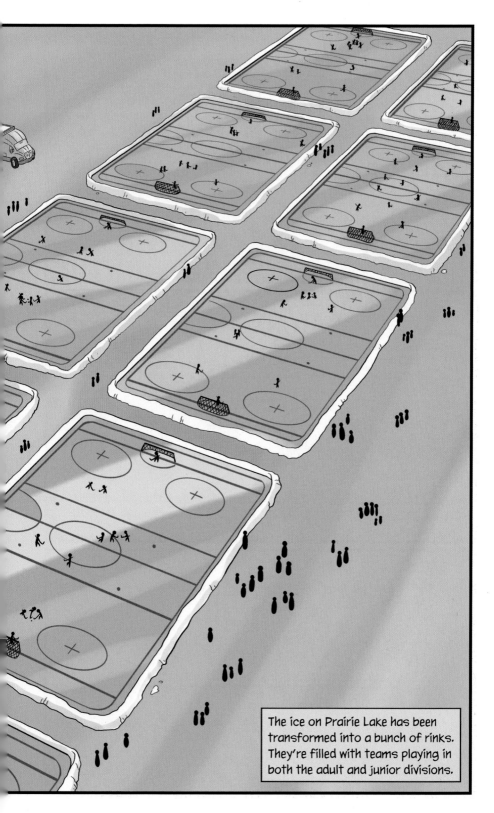

The ice on Prairie Lake has been transformed into a bunch of rinks. They're filled with teams playing in both the adult and junior divisions.

We're all signed in and ready to go.

Cool. Let's find the others.

The rules are simple. Each team has six players. It's a double elimination tournament.

So let's not lose, eh?

One loss will send us to the consolation bracket. But with three wins, we'll be in the championship.

Right! We've got this.

I recognize some of the kids in the tournament. Some are from our school.

Others are from middle schools from neighboring cities—including Raina's beloved Edgewater.

SMACK!

SLAP!

44

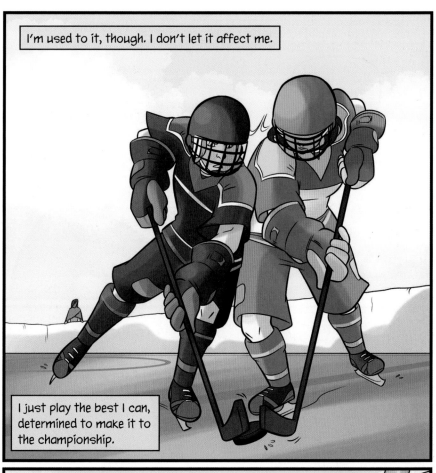

I'm used to it, though. I don't let it affect me.

I just play the best I can, determined to make it to the championship.

WSSH!

FSH!

We win our first game easily, 4-0.

Raina's team absolutely destroys their competition.

That's game! Final score 8-1.

Our second game is tougher than our first. Some of the kids are from Edgewater. They have no problem getting physical, throwing elbows and shoving us around.

Oof!

TWACK! THWACK!

WIZZZ!

WHMP!

If it wasn't for Stella's quick eyes and quicker reflexes, we'd have been toast.

Meanwhile, Raina's team carves up their competition in all three games.

We squeak by in our third game 3–2. But it's official—

We did it!

We're in the championship!

Finally, Raina and I are going to face off against each other.

We've been outside playing all day. We're all tired.

But by the time the sun goes down tonight, the main battle will be won or lost.

Hey Raina.

Sure, Raina's team is older, and bigger, than us.

But I'm not going to let them intimidate me, not here. Prairie Lake is my home ice just as much as it is hers.

Besides, you know how the saying goes . . .

Hey squirt.

. . . the bigger they are, the harder they fall.

Get ready to be schooled on the ice, little bro.

How exciting!

There's Mom and Dad. They're actually watching one of my games. Of course, they're probably just here to cheer on my sister.

It all comes down to this. All the attention and respect I'd been missing.

All the fear of losing my home, my life, my identity . . .

TH4NK!

WHACK!

SMACK!

. . . it all boils down to one hockey game.

But as expected, Raina's team is good. And before we know it . . .

WHOOSH!

CRACK!

They're on the board.

FSH!

Nooo!

Each second seems like a minute. Every minute feels like an hour.

Oof!

They're tiring us out, and they know it.

We need to get our act together.

Or this game will be over by the second period.

Goal!

Then Cora knocks in a goal.

FSSH!

In the third period Izuku slaps in two more goals.

THWACK!

Alright!

We're all tied up!

Time is running out. And so is daylight.

If neither team scores, there's a good chance it'll end in a tie.

And I don't want that at all.

When I see Izuku break away from a defender ahead of me, I pass the puck toward him.

Only—

WHOOSH!

—now you don't.

Raina stumbles, and I spy Izuku still wide open ahead.

Let's try this again.

We carve our way past the defenders, straight toward the goal—

—and one last shot.

THWACK!

GOAL!

FSH!

That's the game! We won!

TWEEP!

I'll take that, thank you very much!

Woo hoo!

We did it guys!

Epic!

Unbelievable.

Epic is right. This feeling? It's great! Indescribable.

It finally feels like everything going on in my life will be okay.

That pond hockey championship is my last great memory on Prairie Lake.

We're moving to the new house now.

We're leaving the only home I've ever known.

It's not easy to leave. But I'll be okay.

Because I've learned so many things. I learned how to stand up for myself, how to be seen, and how to express myself.

65

VISUAL QUESTIONS

1. Extreme closeups help us to better understand
   what a character is thinking or feeling. What is
   Benny feeling in this tight closeup image?

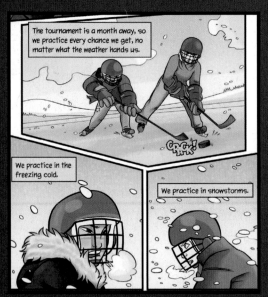

2. Graphic artists
   sometimes use a
   series of panels
   called a montage to
   help tell a story. Look
   at the montage to
   the left. Can you tell
   what is happening in
   the story?

3. Compare and contrast the two similar panels above. What do you think the characters are thinking in the first panel? How do you think they are feeling in the second panel? Why do you think they feel that way?

4. Study the looks on the main characters' faces in the above panels from before the championship game. What do you think Benny is thinking as he faces his older sister? How would you describe Raina's attitude as she faces her brother?

LEARN MORE ABOUT POND HOCKEY

There are many theories about the origin of pond hockey. Some believe it was created by Native nations like the Navaho and Cherokee people.

According to legend, Viking explorers brought pond hockey to Lake Nokomis, Minnesota, in the 1300s. They used a golden shovel to clear away snow on the ice so they could play their favorite game. The shovel was later given as a prize for the winners. Today this tale is known as The Story of the Golden Shovel.

Pond hockey became very popular in the early 1900s. Players cleared snow off the ice on small lakes and ponds. They wore old magazines taped to their legs as shin guards. Teams included just four players. There were no goalies.

The U.S. Pond Hockey Championships was created in 2005. Each year more than 100 teams from around the country come to Minnesota. They compete on 25 different rinks on Lake Nokomis, the same site as the Viking "Golden Shovel" legend.

Thousands attend the U.S. Pond Hockey Championships each year. The champions do not win a prize. Instead, their names are etched into the tournament's own Golden Shovel trophy.

HOCKEY WORDS
YOU SHOULD KNOW

CHAMPIONSHIP—a game or contest that determines which team will win a title

DRILL—a way to learn something by practicing it over and over

FACE-OFF—when the referee drops the puck between one player from each team; the players battle for possession of the puck to start or restart play

GOALIE—a player who tries to keep the puck from entering the goal

INTERCEPT—to stop an opposing player's pass and take possession of the puck

LEAGUE—a group of sports teams that share the same rules

PENALTY—the punishment a player gets for breaking the rules of the game; the player then sits in the penalty box for two or more minutes

POWER PLAY—when a team has a one- or two-player advantage because the other team has players in the penalty box

REFEREE—someone who supervises a sports match or game and enforces the rules

SLAP SHOT—the fastest and most powerful shot in hockey; a player raises the stick and slaps the puck hard toward the goal, putting his or her full power into the shot

GLOSSARY

anchor (ANG-kuhr)—something that provides support and stability for a person or an object

consolation (kon-suh-LEY-shuhn)—a game or match in a sports tournament for teams or players who are eliminated before the final round

district (DIS-trikt)—a zone, area, or region

double elimination (DUH-buhl i-li-muh-NAY-shuhn)—a type of competition in which a team or player must lose twice to be eliminated from play

enthusiasm (en-THOO-zee-az-uhm)—great excitement or interest

intimidate (in-TIM-i-dayt)—to overwhelm someone with superior talent or skill so they become timid or fearful

makeshift (MAYK-shift)—temporary or subsitute

tournament (TUR-nuh-muhnt)—a series of games or matches between several players or teams, ending in one winner

ABOUT THE AUTHOR

Brandon Terrell is the author of numerous children's books, including several volumes in the Tony Hawk Live2Skate, Sports Illustrated Kids: Time Machine Magazine, and Michael Dahl Presents series. When not hunched over his laptop, Brandon enjoys watching movies and TV; reading, watching, and playing baseball; and spending time with his wife and children at his home in Minnesota.

ABOUT THE ARTISTS

Roberta Papalia was born in Catania, Italy, in 1995. After high school, she studied dentistry, but decided to pursue a career in art instead. Roberta studied comic art and animation at Grafimated Cartoon, part of the Palermo School of Comics in Palermo, Italy, and graduated in 2019. Roberta loves to draw and read comics of all types, playing role-playing games, and enjoys several other art forms. Today she lives near Catania with her pet python and two cats.

Jaymes Reed has operated the company Digital-CAPS: Comic Book Lettering since 2003. He has done lettering for many publishers, most notably Avatar Press. He's also the only letterer working with Inception Strategies, an Aboriginal-Australian publisher that develops social comics with public service messages for the Australian government. Jaymes is a 2012 and 2013 Shel Dorf Award Nominee.

Berenice Muñiz is a graphic designer and illustrator from Monterrey, Mexico. She has done work for publicity agencies, art exhibitions, and even created her own webcomic. These days, Berenice is devoted to illustrating comics as part of the Graphikslava crew.

READ THEM ALL!